Anonymous

**Manuscripts in the Charter Chest at Cluny Castle**

**Inverness-Shire**

relating to the Clan Chattan and the Cluny of 1745

Anonymous

**Manuscripts in the Charter Chest at Cluny Castle Inverness-Shire**
*relating to the Clan Chattan and the Cluny of 1745*

ISBN/EAN: 9783337390037

Printed in Europe, USA, Canada, Australia, Japan

Cover: Foto ©Andreas Hilbeck / pixelio.de

More available books at **www.hansebooks.com**

# MANUSCRIPTS

IN THE

# Charter=Chest at Cluny Castle

*INVERNESS-SHIRE*

RELATING TO THE CLAN CHATTAN

AND THE CLUNY OF 1745

EDINBURGH: PRIVATELY PRINTED

MDCCCLXXIX

THE Manuscripts of the following Documents are in the possession of CLUNY MACPHERSON at Cluny Castle. They appear all to have been written in France, probably about 1760, but the writer's name is not known. The first two Documents are narratives relating to the Cluny Family, and of what the Chief of 1745 did and suffered for Prince Charles Edward. The third Document (page 47) appears to be a Petition to the King of France for the royal bounty on behalf of Cluny.

CLUNY CASTLE,
    *October 1879.*

## The Publisher's Preface.

H AVING often heard of the Scots Highlanders as a people remarkablie brave, and
singular in their way; that I read also in our
histories of France, and in most of the histories of
Europe, that the Scots were always esteemed
brave, and that no longer than ten years agoe a
handful of them performed actions which surprised
Europe, I acknowledge I have long had a great
desire to learn something more particular concern-
ing these Highlanders, who had not only drawn
on themselves the observation of the world, but
had likeways raised the apprehensions of the
Brittish Government so far as to oblige them to
make several Acts of Parliament expressly with
intention to disarm them, and afterwards several

other Acts in order to change their dress and their customs.  But my curiosity in that respect was never in any degree satisfyed untill I happened to become acquainted with the Sieur Macpherson, Seigneur de Cluny, chieff of one of their tribs, who, in many different conversations, informed me that they inhabite the large tract of mountains in the north of Scotland which run from the west to the east seas, which surround the island, and likeways inhabite the small islands which ly on the west and north of Scotland, which, in all, may be computed about a third part of the extent of that kingdom.  That their language, which has always been termed Gaulick, and which has no other name amongst them to this day, was once the language of the whole kingdom, untill the course of time, and the immediate connections many of the Scots in low countries with England, by degrees introduced the English language into the lower parts of the kingdom.  They have a tradition among them that their origine was from Sihithia.  Sir William Temple, a very distinct English writer, who was embassador from King

Charles the Second to the States Generall, is of that oppinion, and says that an island in the north of Scotland, wher they first landed from Schithia, took thence the name of Schitland, which it retains to this day ; and that wher they advanced further and took possession of the larger continent, it, for distinction, and by an easie transition, got the name of Scotland. Chevalier Temple's oppinion is further supported by an observation that patrenimicks were from the beginning in use amongst them, and continues still to be so, most tribes having no way to distinguish one person from another but by the name of his father, such as MacDonald the son of Donald, MacGrigor the son of Grigor, MacPherson the son of Pherson, etc. So in Russia and Poland, parts of ancient Schithia, these patrenimicks still continue, such as Peter Alexoivitz, Alexander Petroivitz, etc., which is not knewon to have been the custom in any other countries of the world. Yet others are of oppinion their origine is from the ancient Gauls, by reason that there language was always term'd Gaulick, and that many of their original words have an affinity to the ancient Gaulois. But whatever their origine may happen to have been it is certain they have posses'd that part of the world for so long a time and without any mixture of foreigners, that few countries can, in that point, compare with them. For when the Romans invaded, and over-ran most of Brittain, they found the resistance of. the Highlanders so formidable that they judged it prudent to leave them in the manner they found them. Ever since that time, and how long before non can tell, they have been divided into clans or tribes, each tribe governed by its respective chieff or head of family, and make in all such a body that, if they cou'd be united under one head, from thirty to fourty thousand men might be brought together in a few weeks, and are so formid-able a militia that few, if any, regular troops in Europe could withstand their shock, supposing numbers equall. Their dress, which, as well as their language, continues the same from the beginning, is all woollen, of party colours, consist-ing in a surtout and vest under it, both reaching only down to near the tope of the thygh. Hose of the same, which reach no further up than below the joint of the knee, without any breeches, which are supplied by a plaid girded by a belt round the waste, the lower part whereof surrounds their thyghs, in some manner like a woman's pettycoat, but reach only down to the knee, which is always left bare ; the upper part of the same plaid is fastened to the shoulder, and waves floating round, in some resemblance to the Roman mantle. Their arms are a pistold, and often two, fixed in their belt, a durk or poignard, which they never incline to want, a large sabre slung in the horseman manner from the shoulder, and a fusil, which they generally wear under their arm.

I wou'd have been extremely pleas'd to have, had a distinct account of all the tribes of a people so remarkable, but Mons. de Cluny found himself in no condition to afford me it, yet he entertained me very agreeablie, often with many circumstances of his own tribe, and indeed of his own life, which I found so singular and even so curious, while they were told by him without any ostentation or vanity on his part, that after every conversation

I took notts of it in writing, which, when all were put together, I found would bear printing, accordingly, I resolved to put it in the press, as an entertainment for the curiosity of many, without asking his consent, or even communicating to him my intention; and I hope that when it shall come to his knowledge he will forgive me, having intended no offence to him or to any person; I hope, at same time, no other person can take offence at it, for I'm certain he intended non. I am persuaded that he will find likeways that I have not deviated from the truth of his narration, for I shou'd be greatly concern'd if the publishing of it should even happen to give any shock to his modesty.

THE Sieur Macpherson, Signeur de Cluny,
Chieff of one of the most remarkable clans
of Scotland, is male representative of the Clan-
chattan or Clan-cattan, the most distinguished and
most numberous clan that ever was in Scotland,
and which tradition, handed down from father to
son, and well knowen over all that kingdom, says
came hither from Shithia in a ccnsiderable body,
others say more probablie from Germany, and
landed in the north of Scotland, where two extensive provinces took their names from them, that
of Cathness, or the cat's nest or bay, where they
first landed, and that of Catto, where they afterwards extended themselves; which last mentioned
province, in more modern times, gote the name of
Southerland, to distinguish it from Cathness as
lying to the south of it, but still retains the name of
Catto, in the Galick language, which is to this day

the language of the Highlands, and happened during the reign of the Roman Emperor Tiberius Cæsar.

In these times, and long after, no sirnames were in use, so the clan went by the name of the chieff or leader, and of consequence were named Clan Caten. After having settled in the country they interchanged marriages with the first houses in the kingdom, and several very considerable houses there are of that origine, particularly the honourable and ancient house of Keith, the present representatives whereof are the two illustrious brothers, well knowen in Europe, Signeur George Keith, Hereditary Earle Marishal of Scotland, late Envoye Extraordinary from the King of Prussia to the King of France, and now Governour of the town and province of Neuffchatel in Suisse, with Signeur James Keith, Felt-Mareschal of his Prussian Majestie's forces, and Governour of Berlin, whose predecessor, a son of the chieff of Clan Caton, had distinguished himself in the year 839, when King Kenneth the Second of Scotland conquered the kingdom of the Picks, for his valour on which occasion King Kenneth gave him lands, and dismissed him with the rank of one of the great barrons of Scotland, about which time, by a very small transition, either by accident or with intention to distinguish themselves, their name changed from Chatan to Keith, and their barrony took the name of the family. The representatives of that house of Keith farther distinguished themselves several ages after, about the year 1020, in the reign of Malcolm the Second, by defeating the Danes upon an invasion they made in Scotland, and by killing Camus, their king or leader, at the battle of Barry, in the province of Angus, where the burying monument of Camus is still to be seen, and a village there takes the name of Camustown from it, for which brave action they deservedly obtained farther dignities from the kings of Scotland. So have ever since those times continued to enjoy very extensive lands and possessions in Scotland, and have been always considered a house of great dignity and honour. The house of Sutherland, Earls of Sutherland, whose family name and title are from the province, is likeways very ancient, springs from the same clan, and is term'd in the Gallick language the Earle of Catto, besides several other houses which would be too tedious to mention.

In the year 1291, the chieff of the Clan Catan hapened to have no son, so his only dayghter married a son of Macduff, Thane or Earl of Fife, the then most powerfull signeur in the kingdom.

and made use of his power to carry off the family
lands of Clan Caton in favor of his son who had
married the daughter, and in prejudice of the
male heir, who by some accident had gote the
name of Pherson; various reasons are assigned
for its being given him, but non of them with
such certainty as can be relyed on at this distance
of time. But however it happened, haveing
continued to his death, of consequence his descendants and followers were named Macpherson, which
in that language signifies the son of Pherson, and
which name thus gote by accident the clan still
retains. The son of Macduff, who had married
the daughter and gote possession of the family
fortune was likewise ambitious, and considered it
his greatest honour that the Clan Caton shou'd
acknowledge him for chieff, so with that intention
dropt the name of Macduff, and would willingly
have taken that of Catan. But in those times it
was no easie matter to assume or change a name
at pleasure, for people then were in use to term a
son by the name or some distinguished tittle of
the ffather, so even against his inclination they
continued to name him son of the Thane, which,
in the language of the country is Machk in Dochich,
which name of MacIntosh his descendants and
followers keep to this day. In this manner was

the numberous and ancient tribe of Caten divided
into two great branches, and afterwards suffered
still further subdivisions in smaller trybs of David-
sons, Farquharsons, MacGillivrays, Murdochs,
Smiths, and others, non of whom bearing the
ancient name of Chattan it is now almost entirely
lost, yet the houses of both Macpherson and Mac-
Intosh bear a catt for the cryst of their coats of
arms, with the moto " Touch not the catt but a
glove," which was the cryst and moto of the
ancient house of Caton. Those two houses had
a dispute for many ages which shou'd be the
chieff of the whole Clan Catan, and the matter was
warmly debated before the Privie Councill of
Scotland, at no small expense to both, and no
longer ago than the reign of Charles the Second ;
but the Council wisely reflecting that the name of
Chattan being lost, and the clan divided in so
many branches carrying many different names, it
might make any single house too powerfull to be
esteemed the head and have the direction of the
whole, so disappointed both, and determined that
each should keep his own name and be chieff of
his own clan. But no family ever made any
pretensions to be chieff save those of Macpherson
and MacIntosh. Yet the house of Macpherson,
Signeur de Cluny, is by all the world acknowledged

to be the male representative, and the house of MacIntosh only the female line of the ancient Catan.

The Sieur Evan Macpherson de Cluny, and reall representative of the ancient line of Catan, was born at Cluny in 1707, from his earliest years laid to heart the well-being of his country, and regreted much that it was not improv'd to the degree that it might easily bear. He had long observed that industrie and diligence were greatly discouraged by incursions of louse ungovernable people from different parts of the mountains, who carryed off in droves the cattle of people of all ranks in the lower and better cultivated provinces. The too general calamity gave him real uneasiness, and he was shocked to see those pernicious remains of ancient barbarism reach down to modern times ; he was certain it proceeded only from the remains of barbarism, for he had many convincing proofs that in other respects the disposition of the people in those parts were generally as benevolent, humain, and even generous, as those of any country whatever ; but agriculture having been at all times neglected in those parts, the almost only employment of the common people were in attending their flocks, in hunting and in fishing, which too naturally gave them habits of irregularity and idleness, handed down from father to son, and not easie to be checqued, so he often regreted that earlier pains had not been taken to turn their minds to agriculture and other usefull industrie. He had observed that mankind are generally the same in all countries, too susceptable of being led into bad practices by custom and example, that even in the most civilized governments, besides the precepts of the preacher and the authority of the magistrate, the whipe, the gibet, and the rack, must be too frequently made use of, and even come short in regulating the morals of many, whereas these countries were too far removed from the lash of any of these checks. He had likeways observed that in vice opportunity and conveniency are great temptations, and so great were these in their favours by vast unfrequented mountains, reaching almost in ridges from the west to the east sea, and by their dispersed lonely habitations, that he is convinced if the most civilized society in Europe were established in that country and disengaged from any check on their morals, their descendants wou'd in time be infected, and tempted to make use of the conveniences and opportunities the natural situation affords. The affection he bore his country in general often suggested to him these and such reflections, and prompted him to lay the abuse earnest to heart. But it still affected him more sensiblie when he too frequently observed his own herds, and those of his friends, followers, and dependants, become the prey, which generally landed in the entire ruin of the poorer sort, and in the no small loss of those who were better able to bear it. He determined, therefore, that he wou'd endeavour to put a stop to so pernicious a practice, in so far as concern'd his own lands and the possessions of his clan; accordingly, he rais'd and established a watch or safeguard of his own trustee followers, and at his own and their expense, which for several years had a remarkably good effect over that part of the country where he or his friends and descendants had any possessions. The neighbouring signeurs and noblesse, and even many at a greater distance, such as the Duke of Gordon, Ogilvie Earle of Airly, Stewart Earle of Murray, Gordon Earle of Aboyne, Gordon Earle of Aberdeen, Fraser Lord Lovat, Duff Lord Braco, Brodie Lord Lyon, Forbes of Culloden, Lord President of the Session, Campbell of Calder, Barron Farquharson of Invercald, Sir Ludovick Grant of Grant, The Barron MacIntosh of MacIntosh, The Barron Albert of Castlehill, at that time Sherrif of Inverness-shire, Sir Robert Gordon of Gordonstown,

Barron Rose of Kilravock, Barron Brodie of
Lethen, and Campbell Duke of Argyle, his vas-
salls in the province of Angus, being either all
chieffs of their respective clans or of very distin-
guishing rank in the country, with innumerable
others too tedious to repeat, but however high
their rank was, they laboured still under the hard-
ship of haveing their cattle and those of their
farmers carried off. They were surpris'd at
Cluny's success, and enveyed so much his happiness, that they applyed to him with one accord to
take them under his protection, and cheerfully
offered to join in a voluntary subscription towards
the support and augmentation of his scheme, and
in acknowledgement for his own labour and industrie in a work so laudable and so universally
beneficiall. He listened, and in consequence
doubled his diligence, and his success was in pro-
portion. He never failed to find out and bring
back, even from the most distant parts, all cattle
which from that period happened to be carried off,
in so much that not one single person in the provinces which he had undertaken to protect suffered
in a sixpence, and he also very effectually serv'd
on many occasions even those who had never
applyed to him. The farmers then followed their
industrie in peace and tranquillity, blessing him

in their hearts for the happiness they enjoyed, and every day brought letters full of gratefull acknowledgements from the signeurs and noblesse for the remarkable and surprizing change he had so speedily and so effectually made over the whole country. The subscriptions towards so good a work amounted at that time in his favours to above twentie thousand livres yearly, yet so many were the contributors that it was next to nothing to any particular, and would soon have been very considerablie more by the addition of the Dukes of Athol and Perth, with the noblesse to the southward, and by the addition of the Earle of Seaforth and his clan of Mackenzies, with the Monros and Rosses, and the noblesse to the northward. Yet altho' his success gave general pleasure to most people, it did not fail to draw upon him the jealousie and envy of some particulars, all whom, however, he in a short time reconciled by reason, and by a steady firm conduct, so that those who had been his most inveterate enemies soon became his firmest friends, gaining the good will of all, nor was his name ever mentioned on any occasion but with esteem ; neither does he omitt doing justice to all the clans of Scotland in general, for he affirms that not a single chieff or leading man amongst them but

cheerfully and readily gave him their assistance
in curbing these lawless practices, so distructive as
well as dishonourable, and such was his success in
it that the whole kingdom were witnesses of his
doing more alone in the course of a few years
towards polishing and civilizing the Highlanders
in that respect, than all the power and endeavours
of the Government had ever been able to do by
their repeated tryalls, at very great expense, for
many generations back, in so much that he had the
agreeable satisfaction to see the agriculture of his
own country, which had in all former times been
neglected, augment at least two-thirds in his own.
It may not be amiss to take notice of a pleasant
enough occurrence which happened about this
period, and which afterward became a common
saying in the country. A preacher in the highlands, haranging a numberous auditorie of the
common people in their own language, reproved
them for, and exhorted them warmly against, their
too-well known practices, when to his surprise he
was interrupted by a gray-hair'd reverend-looking
veterane, and an old transgressor, who rose up in
the midle of the assembly and desired him to save
his labour upon that point, for Mons. de Cluny
alone wou'd gain more souls to heaven in one
year than all the priests in the highlands cou'd

ever do in fifty. His reputation in that respect reach'd the ears of the ministrie, who to his great surprise, haveing never once thought of engaging in military or government matters, sent him, to his own house, unask'd for, a commission to command a company in the regiment, my Lord le Comte de Loudin, the same who presently goes to America charg'd with the general command of all the collonies, had at that time authority to raise, and which company wou'd by it advantages have produc'd him at least six thousand livres a year. At same time, the most remarkable signeurs in the country agree'd among themselves, without his knowledge, to solicite the Government that he and his company might have liberty to stay at home in order to protect the country, so that he had reasonable well founded prospects to have enjoyed betwixt thirty and six thousand livres yearly, besides the whole yearly produce of his own fortune, which he found daily improve under his own eye, and whereof neither he nor his predecessors would either know or reap the full value untill the regulations he had lately made enabled him by degrees to do both.

This was his situation, living in peace, in affluence, and in esteem at his own house, at the period the Prince landed in Scotland. The Prince

sent him an invitation to join him with his
followers, and as his principles and those of his
household at all times led them towards a faithfull
attachment to the rightfull royall line of Stewarts,
he did not hesitate in sending back his captain's
commission to the Government in six weeks after
he received it, rais'd his clan, left all, and followed
his Prince, who received him with a hearty
welcome, and with a due sense of his merit.   He
from that time accompanied the Prince through
all his fatigues during the long course of a severe
winter campagne, during which he had frequent
opportunities to observe and be much pleased
with many great quallities in so young a Prince.
In deliberations he found him ready, and his
oppinion generally best; in their execution firm,
and in secrecy impenetrable; his humanity and
consideration show'd itself in strong light even to
his enemies, whom he cou'd not help still to consider subjects, and as he us'd to say, his countrymen.   In application and fatigues non cou'd
exceed him.   Dress'd like a highlander he march'd
on foot at the head of his army from Ed$^r$  to
Derby, at least 300 miles by the root taken,
sometimes 20 miles a day, often over mountains
of heath, in snow and rain; nor was any single
person in his army so alert, never failing to be on

foot in the morning before the appointed hour, and by his own example giving life and motion to the whole, in so much that Mons. de Cluny's attachment to the house of Stewart was very soon augmented by a personal veneration and esteem, and in the return of the army from England, Cluny at the head of his own single clan attack'd the Duke of Cumberland and his cavalrie at Clifton, near Penrith, and repuls'd them with great loss, on which occasion my Lord George Murray, lieutenant-general, who had the command off and brought up the rear of the army, gave the orders, went on with Cluny and fought sword in hand on foot as keenly as a common soldier. The other actions of the Prince and his army are well knowen to the world. Cluny never failed his share in all of them, untill the fatal battle of Culloden, on the 16th April 1746, dispers'd the whole, and obliged every single man in it to shift for himself. The Prince then retired privately to the Western Islands, where he dayly ran great risques of being discovered and apprehended by those who earnestly sought his life. But Cluny, trusting to the faithfull attachment of his people, went directly to his own country, where he found means to conceal himself in safety, as well as Donald Baron Cameron, Lord Locheil, who had been severely wounded at Culloden, and believing himself far from safe in his own country which was too open to the enemy, came to Cluny for protection, accompanied by Sir Stewart Threpland, who with great attention acted both the part of a phisitian and surgeon to him, as did severall others of the Prince's faithfull friends, who happened to be strangers in that part of the world, to all whom Cluny afforded entertainment and security in their greatest distresses. Soon after he had the mortification to see his own house of Cluny, which he had not long before built from the ground with great attention, care, and expense, as a seat for his family, and was by much the best in these parts of Scotland, all in flames by Cumberland's orders. Nor was that his only mortification, for his lady, only daughter of Lord Lovat, who lost his head the year after on Tower Hill for the same cause, with his young family, were thereby turn'd out to the inclemency of the weather, without knowing where to put their heads in safety ; and a worthy father who in the 1715 had acted the same part the son did in the 1745, unable to bear at his years the misfortunes of his royall master, of his country, and of his own family, grieff brought his gray hairs to the grave in a month after. Those melancholly

circumstances were soon followed by others of the
same kind, for he had the grieff to be spectator,
from the mountains and woods, of his country
being ravaged more than once by the military,
many of his own farms and those of his friends
reduced to ashes by fire, their cattle and other
effects carried off beyond a possibility of being
recovered, yet still he was far from being discouraged, nor ever lost hopes, believing firmly
that providence wou'd sooner or later send relieff
and put an end to oppression. But forseeing at
same time that no relieff cou'd happen soon, he
thought of regulating his manner of living. He
had a certain number of a faithfull watch who
always attended him and waited his orders; by
their means he and such as were with him were
supplied in provisions, by their means he kept
a correspondence with his friends, and by their
means he had dayly intelligence of what passed
even in the enemie's camps which lay round
him in the neighbourhood. In this manner he
spent the summer, and about the beginning of
August, to the great satisfaction of all who wish'd
the cause well, he was again joined by the Prince,
who from the time they had parted had undergone
innumerable hardships, had been almost dayly
traced and pursued from place to place, often

faint with hunger and fatigue, often without sufficient cloaths to defend him from the cold damps,
and still oftener without a shoe on his foot. But
after many miraculous escapes, having at last reach'd
Cluny, who had Lord Lochiel with him, he then
found a retreat which might be considered safe, a
comfortable bed and plentie of provisions, which
made so great a difference from his late uncomfortable way of life, that he chearfully used to say Cluny
made him live like a prince. In this manner he
pass'd the time in ease, or at least in quietness. No
surmise or notice was ever so much as hinted of
the place of his retreat, nor a single person ever
appear'd to disturb him. In so much that the
Government, who never slackened their earnest-
ness to find him out, having quite lost the least
information, were making keen searches and en-
quiries about him in countries and at places hun-
dreds of miles distant from where he then happened
to be. The season however advanced, the nights
became long and cold, so Cluny became anxious
for a more comfortable residence for the Prince
dureing the winter, in the event that no better
fate shou'd befall him. He accordingly laid a
plan for that purpose, which he directly caused
execute, and communicated to the Prince; who
haveing long entertained earnest thoughts of

means to get beyond sea, pleasantly answered
that his plan would do very well for a last resource. But happily about the middle of September notice came to Cluny that some ships
were arrived from France in search of the Prince ;
he urg'd his speedy departure, afforded him guids,
provisions, and everything necessary for a considerable land journey he had to make on foot
towards the place where the ships attended, and
which he reached on the 19th day of September.
Lord Locheil, his broy$^r$ Archibald Cameron, collonel of Infantrie in the Spanish service, who was
executed at London in June 1753, Macdonell of
Lochgarrie, present lieutenant-collonel to the Scots
Regiment of Ogilvie, in the service of France,
with several others, attended the Prince beyond
seas, and were thereby relieved of their fatigues
and dangers. But on Cluny he laid his commands to stay in Scotland, both by word and in
writing, as the only person in whom he cou'd
repose the greatest confidence ; assureing him that
he shou'd pay him a visit soon in a way better
supported than formerly, and that at no rate he
shou'd leave the country to such time as he shou'd
see himself, or at least have orders to that purpose under his own hand. Cluny, who well knew
the dangerous situation, wou'd willingly have ex-

cused himself, and have accompanied him along
with the others to France. But the Prince being
urgent he obeyed, trusting to providence and a
good cause, and was willing to risque everything
rather than fail in his duty. The Prince took
accordingly his departure, and arrived safely in
France, whereof Cluny had the agreeable nottice
by the voice of fame soon after. Long afterwards
did he impatiently look for the promised visit,
but to his great grieff it never happened; at last
he had messages from the Prince that he had been
disappointed in his intended return to Brittain,
and that, being entirely sensible of his faithfull
attachment, it gave him real concern that it was
not in his power to provide for him in the manner
he wished, but that, in the meantime, haveing
obtained a regiment from the King of France in
favours of Lord Locheil and his family, he had
named him lieutenant - collonel, which wou'd
afford him about five thousand livres a year, as
small bread for him and his family to such time
as it might be in his power to do more for him.
But still that he behooved to remain in Scotland,
and that his appointments wou'd be paid him from
the establishing of the regiment as faithfully and
punctually as if he were in France. Cluny complyed with no small reluctance, and in consequence

of his obedience underwent innumerable hardships
for a course of nine tedious melancholly years;
woods, mountains, and caves were generally his
best lodgings, and the depth of night the only
time of his movements. The Government were
solicitous to find him out, and for that purpose
troops were dayly employed in keen warm searches
after him; garrisons continually lay in his country,
using every means to obtain informations about
him both by threats and promises; even large
sums and high preferments were repeatedly offered
to any person who wou'd make the least discovery;
yet so remarkable was the attachment of his
people, and the great good will of his other
countrymen, together with his own prudent conduct and directions, that it never was in the power
of the Government for any premium to trace him
so much as one single step, or to discover where
he lodged one single night, which affords an
instance of a private person standing out against
the violent resentment of an enrag'd powerfull
Government for so long a course of time as no
historie or tradition can paralel. In this manner
time passed lonly on from year to year; during
the uncomfortable severity of every tedious winter
he consol'd himself with hopes of relieff in the
spring or summer, but to his grieff he even then

found his hopes disappointed and another melancholly winter overtake him. Here justly may be
observed the effects of habite on the humane constitution, for during the course of nine years in a
remarkablie cold climate, Cluny never once put on
a pair of breetches, or a pair of gloves on his
hands, nor scarce ever found he had use for them,
while at the same time he scarce cou'd ever have
the conveniency of a fire.

His family fortune had been taken possession of
by the Government from the fatal day of Culoden,
but as estates of that kind had always upon such
former occasions been by time brought to a
publick sale, his friends encourag'd him with
hopes that it shou'd be purchased for account of
his family. Yet beyond all precedent, and to his
lasting concern, resolutions were taken by Parliament to annex it unalienably to the crown, and he
thereby deprived of all prospects of recovering it,
even his relations who possessed part of it were
severely oppress'd from no other motive than the
heat of the Government's resentment against him,
and altho' he has now been ten months in France,
yet twenty-four gerrisons still lie in that country
in the houses of gentlemen of his blood and name,
where they use all the hientous liberties of a
revengefull enemy, and command as masters. At

last, in the beginning of May 1755, the Prince's orders to come abroad, wrote by his own hand, reach'd him ; which, tho' they mortified him in one respect, by convincing him that the hopes of a restoration were at a greater distance than he wished, yet he obeyed with pleasure, in regard that continued fatigues and hardships had greatly impaired his health, and an advancing age made him less quallified to suffer more. He accordingly sett out directly, happly made his way, and arrived in France the beginning of June. He then never doubted but that his lieutenant-colonel's appointments would afford him and his family some reasonable subsistence, and that the punctual payment of the arrears which were due him upon it wou'd put him in condition to cleer some debts he had been obliged to contract, and provide him and them in becoming necessaries suiting their rank. But his surprise and mortification cannot easily be imagined when he was inform'd that the only regiment which had been rais'd at the Prince's request had been referm'd immediately after the Prince left France, a regiment which had been granted by the king at the earnest desire of the Prince in favours of the family of Donald Cameron, Lord Locheil, who was the first who sett footing, made figure, and showed example, in the Prince's expedition in Scotland, and without whoes particular active endeavours and appearing directly in his favours with nine hunder of his followers it wou'd never have deserv'd the name of an expedition, and the Prince behooved to have return'd directly to France. Yet he finds this regiment referm'd, and John, the present Lord Locheil, the extremely promising son of a worthy father, and who is well quallified to act the same part in Scotland his father had done, in some respects even better quallified, by haveing earlier knowen the world and languages, not only deprived of all hopes of recovering the seat, and large, extensive, and improveable lands of his ansesters, which can be trac'd back at least 800 years in their family, besides the following of a very numberous clan, but likeways deprived of the very regiment that had been expressly rais'd for the family, and to which his pretentions are but too well founded, and be reduced to act as captain referm'd in the regiment of Royall Scots. By the reduction of the said regiment Cluny finds himself likeways deprived of the far larger part of the bread the Prince believed he had provided for him and his family, and gave him full grounds to depend on. This unexpected shoke bore harder on him than all he had ever hitherto suffered, and made him

almost ballance in his own heart whether he had
not better suffered death in Brittain than live in
France, and see his family and friends in want.
Reason, however, and patience, by degrees took
place, and the school of sufferings which he had
so long been prov'd in quallified him to suffer
more. He then did not in the least question but
the arrears of his appointments of 1800 livres a
year as lieutenant-colonel en suite of the regiment
of Royall Scots, to which regiment he was told he
had been annexed upon the reduction of Locheil's
regiment wou'd be ordered him upon asking it.
Accordingly, he made out a memoire of his request, Lord Lewis Drummond of Melfort, colonel
of the Royall Scots, presented him and it to the
minister, who received both with goodness and
affability, and gave such assurances that he
wou'd soon consider the case as left Cluny no
room to think their wou'd be the least hesitation
in a matter where justice appear'd so much in
his favours that there could be no grounds for
hesitating. He waited an answer for some considerable time with patience; but his patience,
tho' it had been so often tryed, began at last
to weart out, so he then followed the Court,
renewed and continued his solicitations for several
months with no better success; during the inter-

valls whereof he found so much time on his hands
that many anxious reflections intruded on his
mind, even against his inclinations. He cou'd
not help comparing his present with his former
situation ; he saw himself reduced to solicite low
bread at a foreign court ; whereas the time had but
lately been that he wou'd not have moved a step
from his own house for the best regiment France
cou'd afford him, and that no nation in Europe
could put him at the head of a better regiment
than that which his birth and the custom of the
country had given him an unquestionable right to
command. These mortifying reflections were
soon after augmented by nottice being given him
that the minister had all the inclination in the
world to do him service, but that he found his
hands tyed up by rules which admitted of no claim
to arrears by any person who had never join'd his
regiment. He then found himself worse than
ever ; and altho' he did not doubt but these rules
might be right in their foundation, and very
applicable to such as out of folly or wantoness
forbore to join their regiments, yet that being far
from his case, he cou'd not conceive by what rule
either in reason or in justice these rules cou'd be
applyed to him who had been made lieutenant-
colonel of Lord Locheil's regiment, for no other

reason than in consequence of his ready obedience
to his Prince's commands. In consequence of his
obedience to the same commands he stayed in
Scotland, and was thereby absolutely debar'd from
haveing it in his power to join the regiment, and
in obeying these commands underwent a continued nine years' compagne of hardships and
sufferings, beyond comparison severer than any
officer in the French service cou'd possibly have
occasion to undergo even during the warmest
war, so that it may easily be conceived his stay
was no choice in him : for so obnoxious are he
and his followers to the Government that to this
hour they continue their searches for and resentment against him, scarce allowing themselves to
believe that he has left the country, or that, if he
has, he may not still return during these times of
disturbance and give them more trouble than
ever. He is conscious that the Prince well knows
his zeall and that of his followers, as well as their
sufferings, and that if it were in his power to provide for them he wou'd allow non of them to be
in want. He readily agrees that disobedience to
commands deserves punishment ; but to his surprise his punishment comes from giveing a ready
obedience to the person who he believes had the
best and only right to command him, particularly

while he remained in Scotland. At last, however, after eight months' attendance and almost daily solicitations, notice was given him by my Lord Clare that the minister had condescended to give him 6000 livres by way of gratification, out of the extraordinarries of war, but even that not to be payed him to such time as he shall join the regiment; from which time, and not till then, was to have access to the course of his pension of 1800 livres. He acknowledges himself under so great obligations to my Lord Clare that he never mentions his name without all the warmness of gratitude, beleiving he ows even the 6000 livres to his sympathysing disposition and endeavours, tho' at same time it scarce exceeds a third part of his well-founded claim, and still its not being payed him while at Paris leaves him in as great straits as ever. By a nine months' stay and solicitations he had contracted debt to near the value, and is still obliged to contract more before it can be in his power to put himself in a condition to join the regiment. But yet necessity behooved to be complyed with, and fate submitted to however hard; so by the assistance of friends he is equipt and gone to the regiment where he is sorrie to find himself tyed down to an unactive, melancholly life, haveing no command, nor the least thing to do ; much the reverse of what has always been his practice. But what affects him most is the present situation of a deserving lady, with whom he has long lived affectionately in great ease, in plentie, and in honour, with perhaps a hundred servants attending their commands, now reduc'd to live in a cottage in Scotland, with her young family continually disturb'd with a captain's command of the military, one of the 24 garrisons before mentioned, as speys on her, and he so far from being in a condition to bring her or them hither, or to support them if brought, that he finds 1800 livres of appointments, which by retentions scarce exceeds 1600, with difficultie will allow himself bread, without affording a single servant to clean his shoes.

Before concluding, perhaps the reader would be anxious to have some short account of Bade-nach, the country in which Clunie's estate lies, and in what manner the Prince lived while there. Its name Badenach signifies, in the language of the country, bushes of wood, by which the face of it in former times was mostly covered. It lies in the province of Inverness, about mid-way betwixt the east and west seas by which the island of Brittain is surrounded. It is computed from 28 to 30 miles in length east and west, and in some places 18 to 20 in breadth south and north, mountains and valleys included, each of which computed miles may be considered near a league in France. It is inhabited mostly by his clan and followers, who are generall observed by strangers to be the talest and most robust men in Scotland. Somewhat to the westward of the centre of this country was the seat of the family, the Chateau de Cluny, now reduced to ruins by Cumberland, is situated in an agreeable manner on a rising ground, on the north bank of the river Spey, which traverses the country from west to east, the south front of the chateau overlooks the river, makeing many delightfull serpentine windings along several miles of the largest beautifull meadows that are to' be found in these parts. The river afforded salmond and other fishes for his table, the neighbouring mountains and forrests afforded him venison and game of all kinds, and his own flocks and heards boucherie meat at command. Round this chateau, at different distances, were the seats and habitations of his friends and followers, who respected and rever'd him as their common father; with pleasure they received his comands, which, from the ties of affection and from a personal esteem they obeyed as a duty. In points of property his decisions were acquiesced in with chearfullness; he was the arbiter of their differences, the reconciler of their animosities, nor was there any one marriage, or a deathbed settlement, believed valid without his approbation.

About five miles to the south-westward of his chateau commenc'd his forrest of Benalder, plentifully stock'd with dear—red, hares, moorfoul, and other game of all kinds, beside which it affords fine pasture for his numberous flocks and heards. There also he keeps a harras of some hundred mares, all which, after the fatal day of Culoden, became the pray of his enemies. It contains an extent of many mountains and small valleys, in all computed about 12 miles long east and west, and from 8 to 10 miles in breadth, without a single house in the whole, excepting the necessary lodges for the shepherds who were charg'd with his flocks. It was in this forrest where the Prince found Cluny with Locheill in his wounds, and other friends under his care. Cluny observed on this occasion an instance of the Prince's never-failing prudent caution and presence of mind. Lord Locheill, he, and the others, advanced to receive him in the respectfull manner justly due his Royal Highness; "My

dear Locheill," says he immediately, "no ill
plac'd ceremony at present I beg of you, for it is
hard to say who may at this moment eye us
from these surrounding mountains."

How soon the joy conceived on seeing the
Prince in safety and in health gave room for
cooler reflections Cluny became anxious about
his future health and safety. He was afraid that
his constitution might not suit with lying on the
ground or in caves, so was solicitous to contrive
a more comfortable habitation for him upon the
south front of one of these mountains, overlooking
a beautifull lake of 12 miles long. He observed
a thicket of hollywood; he went, viewed, and found
it fit for his purpose; he caused immediately wave
the thicket round with boughs, made a first and
second floor in it, and covered it with moss to
defend the rain. The uper room serv'd for salle
à manger and bedchamber, while the lower serv'd
for a cave to contain liquours and other necessaries;
at the back part was a proper hearth for cook and
backer, and the face of the mountain had so much
the colour and resemblance of smock, no person
cou'd ever discover that there was either fire or
habitation in the place. Round this lodge were
placed their sentinels at proper stations, some
nearer and some at greater distances, who dayly

brought them notice of what happened in the country and even in the enemie's camps, bringing them likewise the necessary provisions, while a neighbouring fountain supplied the society with the rural refreshment of pure rock watter. As, therefore, an oak tree is to this day rever'd in Brittain for having happily sav'd the grand uncle Charles the Second from the pursuits of Cromwell, so this holly thicket will probablie in future times be likeways rever'd for having saved Prince Charles the nephew from the still more dangerous pursuits of Cumberland, who show'd himself on all occasions a much more inveterate enemy. In this romantick humble habitation the Prince dwelt when news of the ships being arrived reached him. Cluny convoyed him to them with joy, happy in having so safely plac'd so valuable a charge; then return'd with contentment, alone to commence his pilgrimage, which continued for nine years more. And now, notwithstanding the very great difference of his present situation and circumstances to what they once were, he is always gay and chearfull; consious of having done his duty he defys fortune to make him express his mind unhappy, or so much as make him think of any action below his honour.

THIS not being intended as a historie of the Prince's expedition, the small beginning it arose from, the two surprising battles he gain'd, the taking the city of Edinburgh, capitale of Scotland, the taking the city and citadale of Carlisle, those of Inverness and Fort-Augustus, besides many oy$^r$ smaller advantages, and marching on foot from the north parts of Scotland, carrying all before him, to the city of Derby, a short way of London, where he made the Ministrie and Government tremble, the publick funds fall, for non wou'd buy them, the Bank of England stop payments, and his rival shake upon the throne, in so much that terror seis'd the whole, and shipping was prepared to carry the Prince and Princess of Wales with their young family to Hanover, and kept the field for near nine months against all the powers of Great Brittain, which was assisted even

by a considerable foreign force both of Hessians
and Hollanders, while he was supported only by
so few that at no time his army exceeded six
thousand men; and money, the sinnows of war,
was even wanting to pay these, while at sametime
his rival had the whole treasure of England at
command.   Glorious as these facts are, both for
the Prince and those who assisted him in perform-
ing them, I shall leave them to some other hand
who is better provided in materials, so shall only
mention one action in which Mons. de Cluny and
his tribe haveing been the only performers, and
being a remarkable instance of what the Highlanders are capable off, sufficiently answers my
present purpose.

In the Prince's return from Derby back towards Scotland, my Lord George Murray, lieutenant-general, chearfully charg'd himself with the
command of the rear, a post which, altho' honourable, was attended with great danger, many
difficulties, and no small fatigue; for the Prince,
being apprehensive that his retreat to Scotland
might be cut off by Marischal Wade, who lay to the
northward of him with an armie much supperiour
to what H.R.H. had, while the Duke of Cumberland, with his whole cavalrie, followed hard in the
rear, was obliged to hasten his marches.   It was

not therefore possible for the artillerie to march so fast as the Prince's army in the depth of winter, extremely bad weather, and the worst roads in England, so mi Lord George was obliged often to continue his marches long after it was dark almost every night, while at the same time he had frequent allarms and disturbances from the Duke of Cumberland's advanc'd parties. Towards the evening of the 28th December 1745 the Prince entered the town of Penrith, in the province of Cumberland. But as Lord George Murray could not bring up the artilrie so fast as he wou'd have wished, was obliged to pass the night six miles short of that town, together with the regiment of Mons. MacDonel, Barron de Glengarrie, which that day happened to have the arrear gaurd. The Prince, in order to refresh his army, and to give mi Lord George and the artilerie time to come up, resolved a sejour the 29th at Penrith, so ordered his little army to appear in the morning under arms in order to be reviewed, and to know in what manner the numbers stood from his having entered England. It did not at that time amount to 5000 foot in all, with about 400 cavalrie, compos'd of the noblesse, who serv'd as volunteers; part of whom formed a first troop of gaurds for the Prince, under the command of mi Lord Elchoe, now Comte de Weems, who, being proscribed, is presently in France. Another part formed a second troup of gaurds under the command of mi Lord Balmirino, who was beheaded at the Tower of London. A third part serv'd under mi Lord le Comte de Kilmarnock, who was likeways beheaded at the Tower. A fourth part served under mi Lord Pitsligo, who is also proscribed ; which cavalrie, tho' very few in numbers, being all noblesse, were very brave, and of infinite advantage to the foot not only in the day of battle but in serving as advanced gaurds on the several marches, and in patrolling dureing the night on the different roads which led towards the towns where the army happened to quarter. While this small army was out in a body on the 29th December upon a rising ground to the northward of Penrith passing review, Mons. de Cluny, with his tribe, were ordered to the Bridge of Clifton, about a mile to the southward of Penrith, where, after haveing pass'd in review before Mons. Pattullo, who was charged with the inspection of the troops, and was likeways quartermaster-general of the army, and is now in France, they remained under arms waiting the arrival of mi Lord George Murray with the artilirie, whom Mons. de Cluny had orders to cover in passing the bridge. They

arrived about sunsett, closely pursued by the Duke
of Cumberland with the whole body of his cavalrie,
reckoned upwards of 3000 strong, about a thousand
of whom, as near as might be computed, dismounted in order to cut off the passage of the
artillirie towards the bridge, while the Duke and
the others remained on horseback in order to
attack the rear; mi Lord George Murray advanced, and altho' he found Mons. de Cluny and
his tribe in good spirits under arms, yet the cir-
cumstance appeared extremely delicate. The
numbers were vastly unequall, and the attack
seem'd very dangerous, so mi Lord George de-
clined giving orders to such time as he ask'd
Mons. de Cluny's oppinion. " I will attack them
with all my heart," says Mons. de Cluny, " if
you order me." " I do order it then," answered
mi Lord George, and immediately went on
himself along with Mons. de Cluny and fought
sword in hand on foot at the head of the single
tribe of Macphersons. They in a moment made
their way through a strong hedge of· thorns,
under the cover whereof the cavalrie had taken
their station; in the struggle of passing which
hedge mi Lord George Murray, being · dress *en*
Montagnard, as all the army were, lost his bonet
and wig, so continued to fight bareheaded during

the action. They at first made a brisk discharge of their firearms on the enemy, then attacked them with their sabres, and made a great slaughter a considerable time, which obliged Cumberland and his cavalrie to fly with precipitation and in great confusion, in so much that if the Prince had been provided in a sufficient number of cavalrie to have taken advantage of the disorder, it is beyond question that the Duke of Cumberland and the bulk of his cavalrie had been taken prisoners. By this time it was so dark that it was not possible to view or number the slain who filled all the ditches which happened be on the ground where they stood, but it was computed that, besides those who went off wounded, upwards of a hundred at least were left on the spot, among whom was Colonel Honywood, who commanded the dismounted cavalrie, whose sabre of considerable value Mons. de Cluny brought off and still preserves, and his tribe likewise brought off many arms; the colonel was afterwards taken up, and his wounds being dress'd, with great difficultie recovered. Mons. de Cluny lost only in the action      men, of whom      haveing been only wounded• fell afterwards into the hands of the enemy and were sent as slaves to America, whence severals of them returned, and one of them is now a sergeant in the regiment of Royal Scots. Here soon the accounts of the enemie's approach had reach'd the Prince, H. R. H. had immediately ordered mi Lord le Comte de Nairne Brigadier, who, being proscribed, is now in France, with the three batalions of the Duke of Athol, the batalion of the Duke of Perth, and some other troups under his command, in order to support Cluny and bring off the artilirie. But the action was entirely over before the Comte de Nairn with his command cou'd reach nigh to the place. They therefore return'd all to Penrith, and the artilirie march'd up in good order. Nor did the Duke of Cumberland ever afterwards dare to come within a day's march of the Prince and his army during the course of all that retreat, which was conducted with great prudence and safety, when in some manner surrounded by enemies.

Altho' the Prince, however, acted wonders which astonished all Europe, and thereby had drawen against him the whole British troups from their campagnes in Flanders, also the Hessians and Hollanders above mentioned, yet it was not possible for him to resist so great a force with his small army, and whom he had not even money to pay, nor sufficient arms to put in their hands, neither was he supported by any foreign troups, excepting a very few from France, which joined him towards the end of the expedition, viz., the batalion of Royal Scots commanded by mi Lord John Drummond, which did not consist of full five hundred men, and which, haveing been form'd only that season, cou'd scarce be so good as his own militia, or at least no better, and a few picquetts from the Irish brigade, many of whom had been intercepted and taken prisoners by the British fleet in their passage. So it need be no surprise that the fatal day of Culloden put a period to the whole, and obliged every single man to shift in the best manner he cou'd for himself.

M R. MACPHERSON, Baron of Cluny, a
Scotsman, Chief of the clan of his name,
is so bold as to implore the king's favours, beseech-
ing him to vouchsafe to hear the relation of what
he has done and what he has suffered in the sight
and to the knowledge of all those of his Nation.

He received from his predecessors an inviol-
able attachment to the royal house of Stewart, and
having dispis'd very advantageous offers which
were made him by the Government for himself,
his family, and his clan, before Prince Edward's
arrivall in Scotland in 1745 he took arms and
accompanied him at the head of his clan during all
his expedition.

His R. H., who had advanc'd the length of
Derby, within thirty leagues of London, having at
that time General Wade behind him in the county
of York, and the Duke of Cumberland coming

down to meet him, both with forces infinitely superior to his, was oblig'd to retire. This Duke pursued him with all his cavalry, and had over-taken his rear-guard at Clifton, when the Baron of Cluny fell in upon him sword in hand at the head of his Highlanders, and entirely routed him, which was the preservation of the Prince's army, and enabled it to make a safe retrait into Scotland.

After the unfortunate day of Culloden, the 27th Aprill 1746, which was so fatall to the just hopes of the Prince, the Baron of Cluny retired to his mountains of Badenoich, from the top of which he soon had the displeasure to see his country cruelly ravaged, the houses of his kindred and vassals reduced to ashes, their effects and their cattle plundered and carried off, the castle of his predecessors totally committed to the flames.

His wife, and children in the cradle, were reduced to wander from cottage to cottage, scarcely finding a place to shelter themselves from the injurie of the weather; his aged ffather, vener-able and respected throughout the whole country, soon sunk under the weight of so many misfor-tunes, and he was deprived of this so valuable a comforter in his adversities.

His R. H. had wandered a long time in the mountains and desarts of the western isles of

Scotland, almost always alone or accompyed with some common Highlanders, without cloaths or shoes, often lacking even the most homely subsistance, and in continual danger of falling into the hands of his enemies. At length having got back to the continent of Scotland, he with much difficulty in the month of August joined the Baron of Cluny in his Badenoch hills. He found there, at least, the necessaries that he had for a long time stood in need of, and especially a secure azilum into a hutt of water-willows, which was made up for him, and where he stayed several weeks in so great secrecy that he was suppos'd to be at the same time eighty miles from thence, and where the soldiers made the most diligent searches for his person.

The Baron of Cluny form'd even then a plan by which his R. H. might be kept in safety all winter in his mountains, secure from being surpris'd by those who sought after him ; and having pos'd it to him, he answered, in a tone which denoted his satisfaction, that he reserv'd that for his last resource.

Happyly it was not necessary ; the Prince got intelligence that two French ships were arrived upon the coast for to transport him ; whereupon the Baron of Cluny sent immediately to advertize the Prince's scattered partisans, such as my Lord

Lochiel, Colonel Cameron his brother, and other gentlemen of note that he had concealed amongst his kinsmen in divers places of his mountains in eighteen or twenty miles round. He got them together again about his R. H. in 24 hours' time, and having provided himself with provisions and guides, he accompany him on foot for the space of sixty miles, that is to say, near to sixty leagues French, to the place of his embarkation, the 30th September 1746.

He himself would have wished to attend his R. H. into France, but he commanded him to stay in Scotland, and to wait there till he shou'd hear from him, he obeyed his commands, altho' he foresaw all the dangers and inconveniences to which he exposed himself, and he return'd to his Badenoch mountains.

About a year after his R. H. found means to send him word to remain still in Scotland untill he himself shou'd write to him ; that in the meantime for to help to support himself and his family till he cou'd procure him a more suitable situation, he had caused him to be appointed lieut.-colonel of his cousin my Lord Locheil's regiment in France, which salary shou'd be punctually payed him.

He remained then exposed, both he and his

family, to the most horrid miseries, in perpetual danger of falling into the hands of the troups, of whom there were many detachments night and day in search of him, with positive orders to bring him in dead or alive, and great rewards were promised to any one who shou'd discover the place of his retreat, and at length finding no other means to make themselves easie in regard to him, the officiers of the troups caused proposals of accommodation to be conveyed him, which his loyalty made him always reject with disdain.

He lived wandering in the mountains, lying in the woods, in the caves, and in the rocks, amongst the wild beasts, his fellow inhabitants of those savage places, receiving provisions by some of the most affectionate of his own clan, who found means in the night from time to time to steal away from the soldiers to succour; he struggled thus for nine years consecutively, without almost ever setting his foot within a house, without fire in the hard winters in the north of Scotland, not changing his place of refuge but in the night time, and always afoot, it being impossible to conceal a horse in his places of retreat, during which time his wife dayly suffered all sorts of hard usage and reproaches from the troups.

Parhaps it will be thought that this recital

is exaggerated; nevertheless, his fellow countrymen, and even his enemies, know that it comes
much short of what he really suffered, and the
extraordinary accidents that he has escaped in the
course of these nine years wou'd be subject for a
whole volum. There is perhaps no example to
be found of a man who has been able to remain
so long in a country in spite of all the means that
a powerfull and incensed Government cou'd
employ for to catch him, and at the same time
always in a capacity of rendering important services to his R. H. if the occasion had offered.

In the autumn of 1752, Colonel Archibald
Cameron, who was executed at London the year
after, and Mr. MacDonell of Lochgarry, now
lieut.-colonel of my Lord Ogilvie's regiment,
arrived secretely in Scotland, charg'd with particular orders from his R. H., directed positively to
the Baron of Cluny, by which he recommended
to him over again to remain in Scotland.

At length, in the month of May 1755, he
received a letter from his R. H., wherein he sig-
nified to him his concern for the dangers and
sufferings to which he had expos'd him for so
many years, and enjoined him to take all imagin-
able measures and precautions for to endeavour
to escape and get into France; he complyed with

his orders; found the means to arrive here in the month of June 1755.

But at his arrivall he found that his long absence had made him lose the small resource that his Royal Highnous bounty had procured for him in this country. The Albany regiment, which was supposed to have been kept on foot both in time of peace and war, by the capitulation granted to my Lord Locheil at Fontainebleau the 30th October 1747, had been reform'd after the death of the said lord; and perhaps his Majesty might have kept it up for his family if the Baron of Cluny, his cousin germain, had not then happened to be absent conform to the Prince's orders, and at the continual peril of his head in Scotland, and consequently at too great a distance, and perhaps unknown to this Court, for to represent their misfortunes and their services. The king, indeed, granted a pension to my Lady Locheil, and to her children, but nothing to the Baron of Clunie's lady or children, of whom there was no mention made by anybody.

He hoped at least, as his R. H. had assured him, to be entirely clear'd off for the bygones of his appointments as lieut.-colonel à la suite of the Royal Scots. Notwithstanding, and after having followed the Court for nine months, at the end of which all the favour he obtained was a gratification of six thousand livres, the most part of which he could not but have spent beforehand, and that perhaps after what he had lost and what he had suffered he might have expected to receive from the king's bounty, independent of his bygone appointments, what his Majestie had been pleased to grant to almost all those who had served in his R. H. expedition; he therefore flatters himself his Majesty will not despise his singular misfortunes.

He is personally outlawed; and having entirely lost all the lands and possessions that he had of his ancestors, he has no other resource but in his Majestie's bounty, his salary as lieut.-colonel reform'd being too small and insufficient to subsist him and his family.

The foresaid detachments were continued in the manner formerly mentioned amongst his kinsmen and vassals after the Government knew that the Baron of Cluny was in France, ravaging them with the utmost cruelty and eagerness; being more exasperated against him than any other of his R. H. party, and being bitterly stung that after having dar'd them so very long he has at last been able to escape them. In revenge of which they so inveterately harrass'd and persecuted his wife that she was forced to apply to the most affectionate of her friends, by whose assistance she has found means to get out of their hands, and arrived with her family at Dunkerque in May 1757.

She deserves some attention on her own account if there is any granted to the memorie of those who have been martyrs of their loyaltie, she being only daughter to the late Lord Lovat, beheaded in the tower of London in the year 1746. So she is in the singular case of seeing her father's family and her husband's both ruined for one and the same cause ; and nobody of her name nor of her clan, no more than of the Baron of Cluny's, have since these sorrowful adventures sued for any favour at his Majestie's hands.

*Printed by* R. & R. CLARK, *Edinburgh.*